Mr Grizley's Class ★

Zoe's Problem

by Bryan Patrick Avery illustrated by Arief Putra

raintree

a Capstone company — publishers for c

Raintree is an imprint of Capstone Global Library Limited, a company incorporated in England and Wales having its registered office at 264 Banbury Road, Oxford, OX2 7DY – Registered company number: 6695582

www.raintree.co.uk
myorders@raintree.co.uk

Designed by Dina Her
Original illustrations © Capstone Global Library Limited 2024
Originated by Capstone Global Library Ltd
Printed and bound in India

978 1 3982 5277 6

British Library Cataloguing in Publication Data
A full catalogue record for this book is available from the British Library.

CONTENTS

Chapter 1
The project 7

Chapter 2
A little help 14

Chapter 3
Success 20

Mr Grizley's Class ★

Cecilia Gomez

Shaw Quinn

Emily Kim

Mordecai Foster

Nathan Wu

Ashok Aparnam

Ryan Clayborn

Rahma Abdi

Nicole Washington

Alijah Wilson

Suddha Agarwal

Chad Werner

Semira Madani

Pierre Boucher

Zoe Charmichael

Dmitry Orloff

Camila Jennings

Madison Tanaka

Annie Barberra

Bobby Lewis

CHAPTER 1

The project

Zoe stared at the pile of string and beads on her desk.

"I'll never finish this," she thought.

"What is all that?" Madison asked.

"It's supposed to be my number line project," Zoe said.

Madison frowned. She pulled a long string with different colour beads out of her bag.

"Shouldn't it look like this?" Madison asked.

Zoe nodded.

"Wasn't that due last week?" Madison asked.

Zoe nodded again.

"I needed some extra time," she said. "I want it to be perfect."

The bell rang for break time. Zoe put up her hand.

"Can I please stay in?" she asked Mr Grizley. "I'd like to work on my project."

Mr Grizley looked at the pile on Zoe's desk.

"I have some things to do here in the classroom," he said. "Yes, you can stay."

Mr Grizley went back to working at his desk. Zoe looked at her project.

"Okay," she said. "Let's get started."

Zoe untangled the string.
She sorted the beads by colour.

She sorted the beads by size.

She sorted the beads by shape.

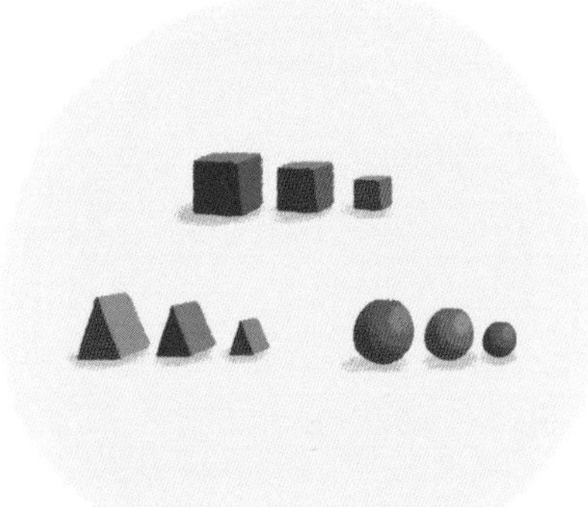

Then, Zoe sighed and stood up. "I think I'll go outside after all," she told Mr Grizley.

Mr Grizley looked at Zoe's desk.

"Before you go," he said, "will you please help me with something?"

CHAPTER 2

A little help

Zoe followed Mr Grizley to the back of the classroom. He pointed to a big box.

"Will you help me carry this into the cupboard?" he asked.

Zoe grabbed one end of the box. Mr Grizley grabbed the other.

"One, two, three, lift!" Mr Grizley said.

They carried the box and put it down in the cupboard.

Mr Grizley walked Zoe back to her desk. “How’s the project going?” he asked.

“I’ve almost finished,” Zoe said. She looked at the piles of beads and string. “I think.”

“I’m sure it will turn out just fine,” Mr Grizley said.

“I want it to be perfect,” Zoe said.

Mr Grizley smiled. “In that case, I’m sure it will be perfect,” he said. “And thanks again for your help with the box.”

"You're welcome," Zoe said. "But you didn't need my help. The box was really light."

"We can always use a little help," Mr Grizley said. "We just have to remember to ask for it."

Zoe looked at the mess on her desk.

"You're right!" she said. "Maybe it's time for me to ask for help."

BE

CHAPTER 3

Success

The bell rang. The children came back into the classroom.

"Did you finish your number line?" Madison asked Zoe.

"Not yet," Zoe said. "I think I need some help. I'm just not sure how to start. Will you help me?"

Madison nodded.

"I'd love to," she said.

"I can help too," Bobby said. "The number line was my favourite project."

At lunchtime, the three friends sat at Zoe's desk. Zoe got out her supplies.

"I want my number line to be perfect," she said. "But I can't decide which beads to use."

Bobby looked at the pile of beads.

"Isn't blue your favourite colour?" he asked. "Let's use the blue beads."

Madison helped Zoe gather up the blue beads.

"We need twenty beads," Madison said.

"But they're all different sizes and shapes," Zoe said. "Won't that look strange?"

"That's okay," Bobby said. "It will make your number line look unique."

With her friends' help, Zoe put each bead on the string. She tied each end.

Zoe carried her project to Mr Grizley's desk.

"This looks great!" Mr Grizley said.

Zoe smiled at her friends.

"Mr Grizley was right," she said. "I just needed to ask for a little help."

LET'S MAKE A NUMBER LINE

In the story, Zoe and her classmates use beads and string to make a number line. You use a number line to practise adding and subtracting numbers. For this activity, we'll make a simple number line that goes from zero to ten.

WHAT YOU NEED:

- string
- 11 beads (any kind of bead will work as long as they fit on the string)
- black marker pen

WHAT TO DO:

1. Cut your piece of string so that it is long enough for eleven beads to fit on it. Leave enough string on each end so that you can tie a knot to hold the beads on the string and so there is enough space to move the beads on the string.

2. Put the beads on the string. You can use any colours, shapes or sizes you like.

3. Tie a knot on each end of the string. Make sure the knot is thick enough to stop the beads from falling off.

4. Lay your number line on a flat surface. With the marker, write the number 0 on the bead on the left. Going from left to right, write the number 1 on the next bead, 2 on the bead after that, and so on. The final bead should be 10.

Your number line is finished! Use it to add and subtract. For example, to add 5 and 3, find the bead marked 5 on your number line. Count three beads to the right and find the number on that bead. In this case, it will be 8. You'll know that 5 + 3 = 8. Always remember: to add, move from left to right. To subtract, move from right to left. As your maths skills grow, you can add beads to your number line or even create a new one.

GLOSSARY

cupboard a space used for storing things

favourite person or thing you like best

project task or problem

sigh take a deep breath as a sign of feeling tired, sad or relieved

unique special or unlike any other

TALK ABOUT IT

1. Why do you think Zoe had such trouble finishing her project?
2. Have you ever found it hard to complete something? What did you do?
3. Mr Grizley asked for Zoe's help carrying a very light box. Why do you think he did that?

WRITE ABOUT IT

1. Have you ever been asked to help someone else? Write about it.
2. Some people have difficulty asking for help. Why do you think that is? Write a paragraph.
3. Pretend you are Zoe and write a thank you note to your friends for helping with your number line.

ABOUT THE AUTHOR

Bryan Patrick Avery discovered his love of reading and writing at an early age when he received his first Bobbsey Twins mystery. He writes picture books, chapter books and graphic novels. He is the author of the picture book *The Freeman Field Photograph*, as well as "The Magic Day Mystery" in *Super Puzzletastic Mysteries*. Bryan lives in northern California, USA, with his family.

ABOUT THE ILLUSTRATOR

Arief Putra loves working and drawing in his home studio at the corner of Yogyakarta city in Indonesia. He enjoys coffee, cooking, space documentaries and solving the Rubik's Cube. Living in a small house in a rural area with his wife and two sons, Arief has a big dream to spread positivity around the world through his art.